KU-723-414

PUFFIN BOOKS

Published by the Penguin Group: London, New York, Australia, Canada, India,
Ireland, New Zealand and South Africa
Penguin Books Ltd, Registered Offices: 80 Strand, London WC2R 0RL, England

puffinbooks.com

First published by Hamish Hamilton 1985
Published in Puffin Books 1995
This edition published 2010
10 9 8 7 6 5 4 3 2 1
Text copyright © Sally Grindley, 1985
Illustrations copyright © Anthony Browne, 1985
Made and printed in China
ISBN: 978–0–141–33160–7

KNOCK
KNOCK
Who's There?

by SALLY GRINDLEY

Illustrated by ANTHONY BROWNE

PUFFIN

KNOCK KNOCK
Who's there?

I'm a great big GORILLA
with fat furry arms
and huge white teeth.

When you let me in,
I'm going to hug your breath away!

Then I WON'T let you in!

KNOCK KNOCK
Who's there?

I'm a wicked old WITCH
with a long pointed hat
and a wand full of magic.

When you let me in,
I'm going to turn you into a frog!

Then I WON'T let you in!

KNOCK KNOCK
Who's there?

I'm a very creepy GHOST
with a face as white as a sheet
and chains that go jangle and clank.

When you let me in,
I'm going to SPOOK you!

Then I WON'T let you in!

KNOCK KNOCK
Who's there?

I'm a fierce scaly DRAGON
with smoke up my nose
and fire in my mouth.

When you let me in,
I'm going to cook you for my tea!

Then I WON'T let you in!

KNOCK KNOCK
Who's there?

I'm the world's tallest GIANT
with eyes like footballs
and feet like a football pitch.

When you let me in,
I'm going to tread on you!

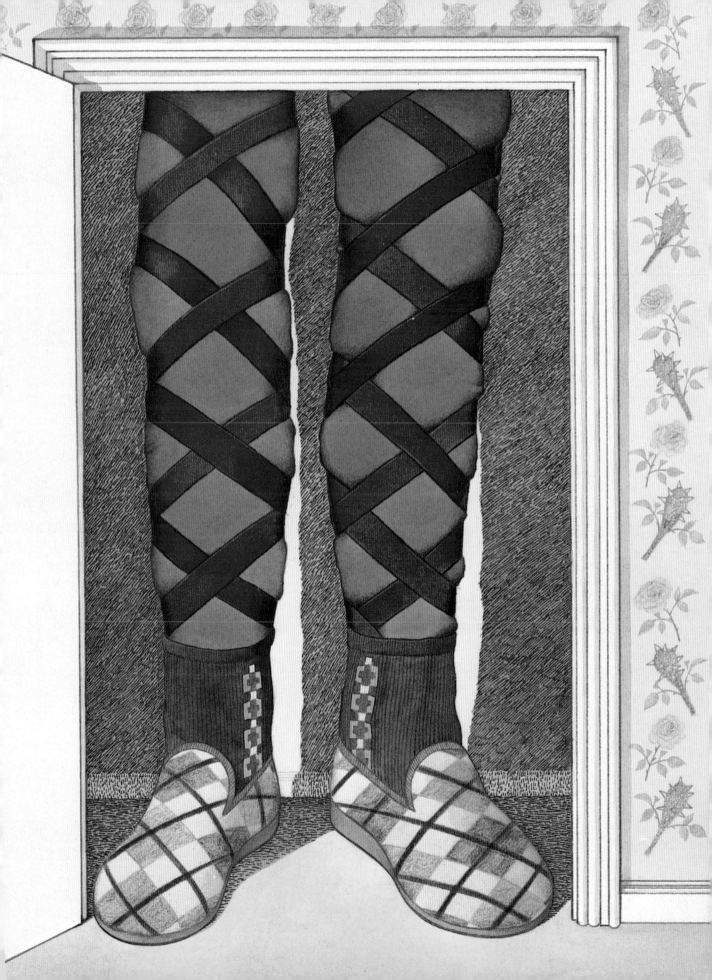

Then I WON'T let you in!

KNOCK KNOCK
Who's there?

I'm your big cuddly daddy
with a mug of hot chocolate
and a story to tell.

PLEASE may I come in?

COME IN, COME IN, COME IN,

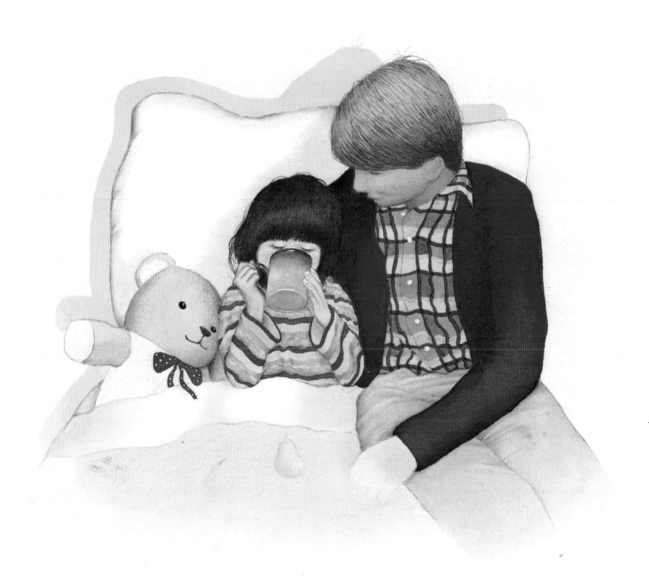

There's been a gorilla at the door,
and a witch
and a ghost
and a dragon
and a giant
and . . .

I knew it was you . . . really.